Lochie's little lie

Hachette UK's policy is to use papers that are natural, renewable and recyclable products and made from wood grown in well-managed forests and other controlled sources. The logging and manufacturing processes are expected to conform to the environmental regulations of the country of origin.

Orders: please contact Bookpoint Ltd, 130 Park Drive, Milton Park, Abingdon, Oxon OX14 4SE. Telephone: +44 (0)1235 827827. Fax: +44 (0)1235 400401.
Email education@bookpoint.co.uk
Lines are open from 9 a.m. to 5 p.m., Monday to Saturday, with a 24-hour message answering service.

You can also order through our website:
www.hoddereducation.com

ISBN: 9781510481671

© Quirky Kid 2020

First published in 2016 as The Best of Friends ™ © Quirky Kid

Concept by Dr Kimberley O'Brien

Illustrations by Connah Brecon © Quirky Kid 2020

Story by Barbara Gonzalez © Quirky Kid 2020

Art direction by Leonardo Rocker

Graphic design by Lisa Diebold

This edition designed and typeset by Gary Kilpatrick

Printed in India

This edition published in 2020 by
Hodder Education,
An Hachette UK Company
Carmelite House
50 Victoria Embankment
London EC4Y 0DZ
www.hoddereducation.com

Impression number 10 9 8 7 6 5 4 3 2 1

Year   2024 2023 2022 2021 2020

A catalogue record for this title is available from the British Library.

MIX
Paper from responsible sources
FSC™ C104740
FSC
www.fsc.org

Lochie's little lie

Activities by
Dr Kimberley O'Brien

Story by
Barbara Gonzalez

Illustrated by
Connah Brecon

Welcome to PYP Friends!

Meet the four friends who live on Quirky Lane and follow the stories of how they

resolve conflict and strengthen their friendships

in the school playground and local neighbourhood.

Salma

Coco

Lochie

Rafi

QUIRKY LANE

"I'm sooo hungry," groaned Rafi.

"Seriously? We just had breakfast!" Lochie couldn't believe Rafi's appetite sometimes.

The boys were on their way to Mr Wozniak's annual garage sale. They loved **rummaging** through his junk in search of new games. This year, Lochie was very excited because he had his birthday money to spend.

"Hey Rafi! Lochie!

Over here!"

called Coco.

The girls were already at the garage sale, trying on silly hats. Just then, Coco saw something very special.
"Wow," she said, picking something up from the table.

"I can't believe it!"

"It's a Magna 720 Game Box and it hasn't even been opened!"

"Awesome," said Rafi and Lochie at the same time.
"Look! There's even a disk for it!" cried Coco. "Planet Racers 3!"

"Excellent!"

they all said.

Lochie couldn't believe his luck. This was the perfect thing to buy with his birthday money. "I'm going to ask how much it is," he said. Lochie took the box from Coco and wandered over to Mr Wozniak.

"Hey Lochie!

Wait!"

... called Coco, a little **annoyed**. After all, she had found the game first and she wanted to buy it. Meanwhile, Lochie was asking Mr Wozniak the price. "How about twenty dollars?" said Mr Wozniak.

Just then, Coco joined Lochie at Mr Wozniak's table.

"How much is it?" she asked. "It's twenty dollars," replied Mr Wozniak. "Oh," Coco sighed. She didn't have enough money.

"Don't you have enough money Coco?" asked Lochie. "No," she replied. "But hang on, I'll go and see if Salma or Rafi can lend me some money."

• • •

Luckily, both Rafi and Salma were happy to give Coco some money.

"Thanks so much!" she called to them and she ran back over to Mr Wozniak to buy the game.

But it was too late.

At that moment, Coco saw Lochie walking off towards his house, with the Magna 720 and Planet Racers 3.

"Lochie!' she shouted. "I was just about to buy that!"

Turning back, Lochie said, "Sorry Coco, but I thought you didn't have enough money."

"I told you I was getting some money from Rafi and Salma!"

Lochie paused.

He didn't know what to say

because the truth was, he knew Coco had gone to get money, but he had wanted the game for himself.

"Oh Coco, I didn't think you were going to borrow some money. Anyway, I had my birthday money and it was just the right amount."

"Come on Lochie, you know I found the game first. You shouldn't have bought it for yourself," said Coco.

"It's not fair."

The words rang in his ears.

He knew deep down that it hadn't been fair of him to take the game. What's more, now he'd lied to Coco, he couldn't go back and change things.

So he just said: "Sorry Coco, but it's mine now." And he took the game box home.

L ater that day, Lochie was busy playing Planet Racers 3. He was already at level six when he heard his Mum making lunch downstairs.

"Lunch already?

How long have

I been playing?"

… he wondered to himself. Then he went back to the game.

Meanwhile the others were getting ready to go to the park. "Is that toast I can smell?" asked Rafi as he walked into Salma's house.

"Yep, do you want some?"

"Absolutely," replied Rafi.

"Of course you do," answered Salma, rolling her eyes, "I should have known."

After toast, Salma and Rafi went to pick up Coco. "You're late," she said.

"Sorry, I had to stop for toast at Salma's," said Rafi.

"Of course,

I should have known,"

she replied. Coco and Salma giggled to themselves.

Next, the kids walked over to Lochie's place and knocked on the door. Lochie's mum answered and called for Lochie to come to the door. She called once, twice, three times and finally she went in to get him.

"Lochie, your friends are here. They're going to the park."

But Lochie
didn't answer.

"Lochie, your friends are here!" she repeated, this time quite loudly.

"What?" Mum, I can't do anything right now, this level is really tricky."

"So you don't want to go to the park?"

… she asked.

But Lochie didn't answer again. So his mother went back to tell the others. They all thought it was a little bit strange, but they went to the park anyway.

After the park, Rafi went to visit Lochie who was still on the Magna 720.

"Hey Lochie, how's it going?" Lochie didn't answer, so Rafi tapped him on the shoulder. "What level are you on? Can I have a go?" Lochie pressed the pause button. He wasn't pleased about stopping the game to talk to Rafi.

"What do you

want Rafi?

I'm almost at the next level."

"Er, sorry," said Rafi. "Can I have a go?" Lochie gave the controls to Rafi.

"Hey, why didn't you come to the park with us today?" asked Rafi. Suddenly, Lochie felt annoyed.

His friends had been to

the park   without   him!

"What? Why didn't you tell me you were all going to the park?"

Now Rafi was confused. "What are you talking about? We came to get you but your Mum said you didn't want to go."

"That's not true, you didn't come here."

"Yes we did!"

Lochie had had enough. He wanted Rafi to go so that he could keep playing.
"That's enough now, it's my turn again."
"But I haven't even had a proper turn."
"Too bad."

Rafi was now confused and annoyed.

He'd never seen Lochie be so rude and mean.
"Whatever," he replied. "I have to go now anyway." But Lochie had already taken the controls and was glued back to the screen. He didn't even notice Rafi leave.

Early on Sunday morning, Lochie was making his way to the living room. He had almost reached the last level of Planet Racers 3. As he sat down to play,

he heard his

friends outside.

It looked like they were going to the park so he went downstairs to join them. But when he opened the door, he saw that his friends had walked straight past his house – without stopping to pick him up.

Lochie watched from the window as they walked down the street, feeling confused. He then remembered how horrible he'd been to Rafi and Coco and felt awful.

Suddenly,

he didn't want to play

the Magna 720

any more.

But what could he do?

Would his friends forgive him? Lochie needed some advice, and he knew exactly the person to ask. Lochie explained the whole situation to his dad who listened closely.

"I feel terrible,

I should never have taken

the game from Coco."

"Well, maybe it's not too late to give it back?" his dad suggested.

Lochie thought for a moment.

"Yes! That's it!

See you later Dad, I've gotta go and see Coco!"

Coco couldn't believe it.

"Really? You want to give me the game?"

"Yep, it should have been yours in the first place. I'm really sorry about that."

"Well, that's okay, but I've got a better idea ..."

"How about we all share the game?"

Lochie thought that was a brilliant idea ...

"Come on, let's go tell the others!" said Lochie.

Coco explained the plan to share the Magna 720 between all of them.

Just then, Lochie had another idea. "And how about we promise to play together as often as we can. I think it'll be more fun that way." All the kids agreed that playing together was definitely more fun.

"And one more thing," added Lochie. "If it's a nice day, we should always go to the park first. And ... please don't forget me again."

"No way, we won't forget you.

It's better with you around anyway,"

said Salma.

Lochie's smile couldn't have been wider and he sighed with relief.

He was *so* glad to be back with his friends.

"Well, what are we waiting for? It's a beautiful day, let's get to the park!"

"Yay!"

they all cried.

"Um," said Rafi. "Can we stop for a pie on the way? I'm so hungry."
"Of course you are, we should have known!" they all laughed.
And off they went, via the pie shop.

Role play:

How to negotiate

Finding a solution to a problem by working together is called negotiation. Negotiation is a life skill that will help us in many different situations. It is a way of exchanging ideas and choosing the one that best suits everyone.

Ingredients

LISTENING SKILLS
You need to be able to listen carefully to each other.

FAIRNESS
Being fair to everyone is a good way to find a solution.

PRACTISE
The more you negotiate, the easier it becomes.

FLEXIBILITY
To negotiate, you need to be prepared to 'give and take' and be 'open-minded'.

HONESTY
Be honest about your feelings and be respectful of each other's boundaries.

Method

Step 1

Choose one person to be your partner.

Step 2

From the list below, choose a topic you and your partner would like to negotiate.
☐ What to do on the weekend
☐ Who will feed the dog
☐ What game to play

Step 3

With your partner, discuss some ideas and solutions and their pros and cons.

For example, explain why you would like to play your game first.

Step 4

Write down the things you agree on.

....

....

Step 5

Now, propose a fair outcome to your partner and find a win-win situation together.

Step 6

If you still can't agree on all points, go back to Step 3.

27

Glossary

Rummaging (page 2)
Searching for something by rifling and hunting through things.

Annoyed (page 5)
To feel irritated or slightly angry about something.

Rang in his ears (page 8)
Something that replays in your head and stays in your mind.